To Ben, who painted Tucker pink
*when **he** was a little monkey*
– S S

To Mary
– N S

Copyright © 2009 by Good Books, Intercourse, PA 17534
International Standard Book Number: 978-1-56148-668-7

Library of Congress Catalog Card Number: 2008055866

Text copyright © Steve Smallman 2007
Illustrations copyright © Nick Schon 2007

Original edition published in English by Little Tiger Press,
an imprint of Magi Publications, London, England, 2007

Printed in Singapore

Library of Congress Cataloging-in-Publication Data

Smallman, Steve.
The monkey with a bright blue bottom / Steve Smallman ; Nick Schon.
p. cm.

Summary: In the newly-formed world, monkey uses a paint set to make napping
animals as colorful as birds, even adding stripes, squares, and spots, but when
bear awakens and sees the changes, he makes monkey the most colorful of all.
ISBN 978-1-56148-668-7 (hardcover : alk. paper)
[1. Stories in rhyme. 2. Animals--Color--Fiction. 3. Jungle animals--Fiction. 4.
Creation--Fiction.] I. Schon, Nick, ill. II. Title.

PZ8.3.S6358Mon 2009
[E]--dc22
2008055866

THE MONKEY WITH A BRIGHT BLUE BOTTOM

Steve Smallman

Nick Schon

Good Books

Intercourse, PA 17534
800/762-7171
www.GoodBooks.com

A long time ago, when the world was quite new,
A monkey sat watching the birds as they flew.
Like feathery rainbows they flashed through the air.
"How come they're so pretty?" he thought. "It's not fair!"

All around him were creatures of every sort,
Some fat and some skinny, some tall and some short,
But none of them purple or yellow or blue;
They all looked as dull as an elephant's poo.

The monkey walked down to the stream with a sigh,
Then a vivid blue kingfisher bird darted by.
He followed it down to a gap in the rushes
And there was a paintbox with one or two brushes.

He snatched up the paintbox as quick as a wink,
Tried painting some flowers and then had a think:
"Somebody painted this kingfisher blue,
I'm going to paint all the animals too!"

The animals always get out of the sun
And go for a nap at a quarter to one.
So when he was sure everybody was sleeping,
With paintbox and brushes the monkey came creeping.

He painted some frogs and a couple of snakes
And thought to himself, "What a difference it makes!"
Then feeling much bolder, the cheeky young fellow
Set out to paint a leopard bright yellow.

Just then the big cat gave a growl in his sleep
And monkey shot into a tree with a leap.
The black paint dropped out with a splash from the box,
And fell on the leopard in little black spots.

"That's great!" said the monkey,
   then, just for a laugh,
He painted brown squares on a yellow giraffe,
Black stripes on a zebra and white on a skunk,
And both on the lemur asleep in his bunk.

"Hee hee!" laughed the monkey. "I'm having such fun!"
Then he spotted a bear fast asleep in the sun.
He took out his brush and then, what a surprise,
He painted white circles around the bear's eyes!

Bear woke with a start and yelled,
  "WHAT DID YOU DO?"
Which woke up the rest of the animals too.
The monkey was frightened and practically fainted,
Surrounded by all of the creatures he'd painted.

They all started yelling till bear shouted, "HUSH!"
Then quietly picked up the paintbox and brush.
He painted the monkey's face red, white and blue.
And then for good luck did his bottom end too!

And still to this day when the monkey goes by,
The animals giggle, they laugh till they cry.
His bum is still blue as a bright summer sky,
He looks like a clown – and now you know why!

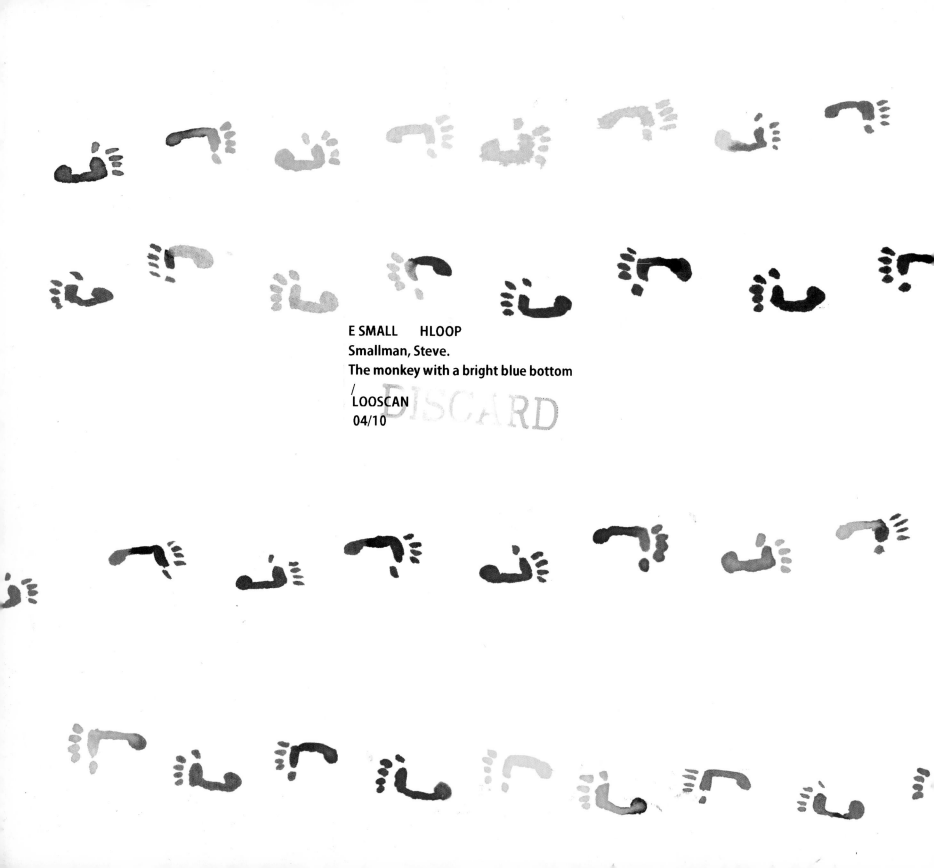